Veronica, I Heard Your Mom's Black

Now that people are making a big deal about her black mother and white father, Veronica's world is changed forever. But how does she find herself in everybody else's confusion? In all the chaos?

Veronica's hair is wild, and no one will shut up about it. Her mother wants to know if her friends "know." She's always been mixed, but now suddenly she's questioning herself.

Her so-called friends are talking about her behind her back—and other people are saying obnoxious things to her face. How will she figure out where she fits in?

Veronica, I Heard Your Mom's Black

Two Sisters Writing and Publishing™
Silver City, NM 88061

www.twosisterswriting.com
www.atkinsgreenspan.com

A version of this book is housed in the Gleeson Library,
University of San Francisco, San Francisco, California.
© 1996 Catherine M. Atkins

For information, contact
Two Sisters Writing and Publishing™
2340 Hwy 180 East, Suite 244
Silver City, NM 88061

Two Sisters Writing and Publishing™
June 2017

Manufactured in the United States of America

Cover and interior design by 1106design.com

ISBN 978-1-945875-00-7
eISBN 978-1-945875-03-8

First Edition

Veronica, I Heard Your Mom's Black

CATHERINE M. GREENSPAN

Two Sisters Writing and Publishing™

Chapter 1

"Veronica, I heard your mom's black..."

Robert Cleary looked down his narrow, pointed nose at me. I stared at the big splotchy freckles covering his otherwise transparent cheeks and forehead.

My heart seemed to pause before it pounded in my chest, in my ears, and in my temples. I took a deep breath and said, "She is black."

No stranger had ever said anything to me about my mother being black. I turned away, hoping Robert wouldn't say anything else.

He tapped me on the shoulder. "Well, if she is—"

I turned fast and stepped forward so my face was within inches of Robert's; I smelled his milky breath. "If she is, it's none of your business."

I stamped my foot and cocked my neck the way I'd seen tough girls, black girls, do, and I squinted my eyes, hoping to look mean. "You better quit talking about me behind my back."

Robert's lips glistened with saliva. "I, I didn't mean anything."

I opened my eyes wide and said, "Then get out of my face."

He stepped backwards away from me, and I stared him down until he turned around and walked away.

I let out my breath. I was sweating under my arms and my heart was thundering. Here I was in eighth grade, my last year of middle school, and now all of a sudden I had to deal with an ugly boy with flaming red hair, who wanted to know about my ethnic makeup as if it were his right.

Back in sixth grade my biggest fear had been getting lost or having none of my friends in my classes. In seventh grade, when my sister Vicki left middle school for ninth grade at the high school, I missed seeing her and her friends in the halls. But now in eighth grade, I wasn't afraid of anything, or anyone.

Or so I thought.

My heart raced all day long. Whenever I saw a redhead, I felt my stomach turn a somersault. I should've punched Robert Cleary. He had no friends! What was he doing talking about me behind my back? About my mother, too?

After school, as I did my homework, I stared at my hands and arms.

White.

White like my father's skin, I thought. The veins underneath looked like a road map. My mother's skin resembled the color of my father's coffee—he put a lot of cream in his coffee. With creamy tan skin and dark hair and eyes, she was beautiful.

That night I tried to get a good look at Daddy and Cap without their noticing. They were always there; I never really looked at them.

I set the table for dinner thinking, *he's a white man and she's a black woman.* I knew that since before I knew I knew it, but why did it matter to Robert Cleary?

Cap and Daddy laughed at some inside joke as they brought in hamburgers and French fries for Vicki and me. I forgot about the boy from school and after a second, I forgot that Cap's was the only skin in our family that wasn't white.

Later we all watched a movie on TV, Daddy on the La-Z-Boy, Vicki and me on the couch, and Cap performing her weekly hair ritual on the floor with her back to the couch between Vicki and me.

3

She had just washed her hair. Then she sat on some pillows with her head under her big, hooded dryer propped on the couch. We turned up the TV as loud as it would go to drown out the hum of the dryer.

After a while, Cap turned off her dryer (and turned down the TV) and went into the kitchen. I followed her, observing that her super-tight curls sprang in every direction from her head, straight up in the air and down to her shoulders.

I got a glass of water while she rummaged for her hot comb in the drawer where we kept the hammer and thumbtacks and maps. When she found it, she set the heavy brass comb on the stove's front right burner and turned the flame up to medium-high. I followed her back into the living room.

The movie had come back on, so Daddy filled us in on what we'd missed, but I paid only half attention. Within minutes I could smell hair and grease being cooked off the comb on the stove.

Cap sat on the couch, working a big, plastic comb through the kinks in her hair. She grimaced as she tried to get her hair to part so she could slather on some blue greasy goop called Ultra Sheen that would protect it from the hot comb.

After she finally finished combing through all the knots, she went into the kitchen and came back with the hot comb. The rubber of its black handle was half an inch thick, so no matter how long she let it sit over the flame, she could always pick it up. She sat back down on the couch, her eyes on the TV screen, and pulled the comb through her hair, ironing away the kinky curls.

The hot comb straightened her hair as thin as paper after she pulled it through only once or twice. When the comb got too close to her scalp, she yelled, "Ooh! Ahh!" but she continued to press her hair until it was all lying flat down the sides of her head, fixed in place and as straight as a freshly ironed and starched handkerchief.

Once or twice she took the comb back to the stove and let it heat up some more before finishing all the sections of her hair.

When she was nearly done, she asked me to run to her room to get her curlers. I gladly participated in her ritual and carried the basket of yellow and purple curlers and bobby pins to her.

"I'll trade you," she said, holding the hot comb out with its rubber handle toward me. I set the curlers down and took the hot comb to the kitchen where I set it on the flameless stove to cool. The next morning, I knew, Cap or Daddy or maybe Vicki or I would put the comb back in the utility drawer with the scissors and screwdrivers and thumbtacks.

Until then, Cap continued her ritual by rolling her hair: big purple curlers on the sides and in back, and little yellow curlers on the top. When she finished bobby-pinning the rollers in her hair, she would put on a scarf and sleep with them.

In the morning she would pull out the curlers then gently brush out the ringlets, leaving soft, pretty curls. She wouldn't need to wash or hot comb it for a week. Some nights, though, she might re-roll the hair on top to give it more body.

She did this every week.

Now I said good-night as she and Daddy continued watching the movie. Lying in bed, I tried to recall if any of my white friends had ever seen my mother's hot comb or if they even knew what one was. Did they have any idea that Cap's hair wasn't naturally curly the way they saw it?

What did my friends think of my hair? Daddy had a rule for Vicki and me: no cutting our hair until we turned eighteen. That had been fine when we were little because Cap took care of it every day, mainly brushing it back with barrettes or putting it into ponytails or braids.

In sixth grade I started taking care of my own hair, which meant I was the one putting it in barrettes or ponytails, but mostly just braids. During the summer between seventh and eighth grade, out of nowhere, my hair went from fine and flaxen to thick and frizzy. Overnight, it seemed, it became as thick as a forest, and I could no longer work a brush through it when it was dry. All I managed was to comb out the kinks and tangles with Cap's wide-toothed comb. That only worked when it was sopping wet, after I slopped a handful or two of conditioner on it.

My hair had once been long and silky, but not anymore.

Victoria's hair changed two years ago when she was my age, but instead of going from straight to bushy like mine, her blonde hair turned into spirals and ringlets. Her hair became super curly; mine became a coarse, shapeless mass reaching all the way down to my waist. And I could not cut it.

One time I put some of Cap's Ultra Sheen on it to make it less frizzy, but that just made it look like an oil slick. It overwhelmed me so much that all I managed each day was to part it straight down the middle and tuck huge bunches of it behind my ears. Or lock it up in a braid.

My hair was no longer white people's hair, but it wasn't quite black people's hair, either. As I tried to fall asleep, I wondered who else besides Robert Cleary was talking about my mother being black. Cap was the coolest mother of all the mothers I knew, so if people were talking about her, they ought to be saying how wonderful and beautiful she was.

Cap was different from my friends' mothers in more ways than just her hair regimen and skin color. For one, Vicki and I had been calling her "Cap" since we jokingly referred to her as the Captain from *The Love Boat*. We had called her "Mommy," still called Daddy "Daddy," but "Mom" never fit her, and "Cap" stuck.

My best friend Katie's mother wore thick, tinted glasses and cut hair and gave permanent waves in her kitchen. Katie called her "Mom."

Katie always teased me when she heard me call my mother "Cap."

"That's so weird," she'd say, but I was sure she meant it in a good way.

My friend Debbie Harrell lived down the street from us with her three little brothers. Her mother had walked out on them in fourth grade. She reappeared in sixth grade and took Debbie out of school in the middle of gym class. Debbie was gone for two weeks then, and we'd peered out our front windows to see the police cars parked in front of the house, wondering what was happening.

When Debbie came back, she told us her parents hated each other and would do anything to hurt each other and that she didn't want to talk about it. I thought she was brave for not crying about it, but I couldn't imagine not having a mother around or having a mother who might kidnap me at any moment just to make Daddy mad.

My friend Susan was an only child whose parents owned a chain of restaurants. They were never home and always made her stay with an aunt or her grandparents. Susan actually yelled and swore at her parents in front of me and our other friends, begging them to let her stay home alone. She always called her parents "the evil couple." She'd never been given a birthday party in her whole life.

The black friends I had at school never invited me to their houses, so I didn't know what they called their mothers. I didn't know any white mothers who were called anything other than "Mom."

I couldn't imagine having any mother but my own—Cap was so fun and young. Cap's uniqueness made me love her and appreciate her.

For the next few days, I walked to school with a stomachache. What if I saw Robert Cleary again and he said something in front of my friends? My friends knew my mother was black because they'd been to my house hundreds of times, but we'd never actually discussed my family's racial makeup.

A few weeks later at lunchtime, Katie and I were walking through the lunch line when a girl named

Maria Richardson said, "Is your mamma black? If she is, you need to sit with me."

She then stood with her hands folded across her barrel chest, leaning all her weight back on one foot with her other hip jutted forward.

I had a frenzy of thoughts. Did she want to be my friend now because she knows about my mother? I was confused and so surprised that I couldn't think of anything to say. Up close, she was very pretty.

Something rose out of the bottom of my insides, up through my stomach, into my throat.

"Well?" Maria asked.

I glanced at Katie, but she had moved forward all the way to the cashier at the end of the line.

She turned and called, "Come on, Veronica, you're holding up the line."

"She is," I said to Maria, staring into her demanding eyes.

"Well, then. You're a sister," she said, relaxing her posture and putting her arm around my shoulder. She started walking, pulling me along with her. "Why don't you come on over here?"

"But, Maria..." I stopped and pointed up at Katie with my lunch tray. "Katie and I are eating together. Do you want to eat with us?"

"No, I don't want to eat with your white-ass friend."

She snatched her arm from around me and walked off into the cafeteria.

What just happened?

I wanted to call out after her, "I'm sorry," but I had nothing to be sorry about.

"Veronica!" Katie called. "Come on!"

I paid for my food and caught up to Katie.

"What did she want?" Katie asked.

"Nothing."

"She must've wanted something. Why won't you tell me? Why are you being all secretive, Veronica?"

I said nothing. Why had Maria called Katie a "white-ass"—just because she was white? Why the hostility?

Just as I checked over my shoulder to see where Maria had gone, Katie turned toward me, our trays bumped together, and hers flew into the air. Her knife, fork, plastic dishes, and food scattered on the floor. The noise echoed in the high-ceilinged room, and I could feel the eyes of everyone on us.

Katie looked at me, her eyes filled with tears. "Oh my God, Veronica. Really?"

A lunchroom monitor appeared and told Katie to go back through the line and tell the cashier she spilled her tray.

"I'll see you at the table, Katie," I said.

Katie curled her lips in a snarl and headed for the line. As I walked over to our table, it might as well have been my tray that spilled.

Everyone watched me. I wanted to lift my tray and say, "Look! It wasn't me! Mind your own business!"

I saw Maria Richardson standing in her tough-girl stance. She glared at me with her lips pushed together. She looked madder at me than Katie had been for embarrassing her in front of everyone.

Katie didn't say a word to me during lunch, but forgave me that afternoon. Maria Richardson continued to give me dirty looks whenever I saw her in the halls. It was the weirdest thing.

I didn't understand why she treated me as if I'd done something to her. I couldn't just abandon my friends and sit with her because she learned my mother was black.

Later that day I saw both Robert Cleary and Maria Richardson in the hall. Suddenly it occurred to me that because Cap was black, I ran the risk of becoming an outcast. Not being entirely white or black was reason enough for one group or both to hate me.

I wasn't that different from the most tormented girl in my grade, a girl named Nona Staharg. Everyone said her parents were nomads, that they weren't from anywhere. Nona had beige-orange skin and short curly hair and eyebrows so thick they grew together like a bushy mustache across her forehead.

Of all the girls with white skin in my grade, my hair was the most massive, the frizziest, the ugliest. In my mind, it drew more attention than Nona's big eyebrow. When I heard that someone had smeared dog poop on Nona's locker, I thanked God it hadn't been me and wondered if it ever would or could be.

So far, none of my friends had mentioned the change in my hair. I expected them to say something; after all, I paid careful attention to their hair, especially the way Katie's and Debbie's straight, fine hair blew in the wind when we were outside, and then settled back when we went back inside. Mine looked like a tumbleweed after a dust storm.

A few weeks after the Robert Cleary-Maria Richardson week of weirdness, Katie's friend Maggie asked out the blue, "Why is your hair so bushy? I mean, I would expect it if you, like, lived in a jungle."

Maggie lived on Katie's block, but I'd never had a class with her, and I never liked her very much. She wore expensive, flashy clothes from a store called Sassy Girl. I didn't know anyone else who shopped there. Cap had taken Victoria and me there once, but we couldn't afford anything, so we just left. No one had asked if we needed help, anyway.

Maggie went out with high school boys and was a finalist in *TEEN Magazine's* model search. She'd been wearing a bra since third grade, and I was convinced it was because she'd been held back. She looked sixteen, not fourteen.

I hadn't worn my hair down in weeks, and now I was getting sudden commentary. I hadn't expected Maggie to make fun of my hair by asking such a mean question.

I looked at Katie, hoping she might defend me by saying something smart or funny since her mother cut hair, but she just kept eating her tuna fish sandwich.

"It used to be straight," I said, reaching up and pulling it back into a ponytail with my hands.

"Yeah, maybe it did," Maggie said, laughing as she bit into a chocolate chip cookie, "but now it looks like you stuck your finger in a light socket."

Everyone laughed. I hated Maggie, pretty clothes, big boobs, hair and everything else about her.

My eyes filled with tears and my throat burned as I tried to smile and laugh along. I had nothing to secure my hair with, so I just held it back with one hand until my tears went away. When I finally let go of my hair, it expanded and came forward over my shoulders.

I'm never wearing it down again, I thought.

No one said anything more about my hair for the rest of the afternoon, but each time I saw someone laughing, I imagined that my hair was their joke.

That night at home, I moped around. When I walked into the living room to watch the eleven o'clock news with the family, Vicki said, "Your boobs are enormous."

I burst into tears and ran to my room. First of all, my boobs were not "enormous." Secondly, Vicki was the last person I wanted teasing me.

I heard Cap and Daddy tell Vicki to apologize. She came into my room and said she was sorry, but I buried my head under my pillow and yelled at her to go away.

That weekend Cap and I went to the mall to buy bras for me. The bra department was right inside the door of Hudson's, so everyone entering the store was able to see us. I felt as if I were going to the bathroom in a stall with no door, right there in front of everyone.

Cap headed for the training bras, but I stayed at the underwear bin looking at the different flower patterns until she finally called, "Veronica, come here this instant!"

A saleswoman approached and asked if we needed any help finding the right size. Cap said no, and we went into the dressing room with the handful of different styles and sizes she'd found. They all made me feel like I had a band of plastic wrapped around my chest. Cap tried to adjust them a little while they were on me, but I couldn't possibly know if I liked one while she stared at me. I didn't even want to look at my reflection.

At one point, I was completely naked from the waist up, switching from one bra to another, when the saleswoman walked into the dressing room and practically shouted at us, "How're we doing?" The door only came up to her shoulders, but Cap stood up quickly to block me from the lady's view of me. I pulled my arms up to my chest quickly.

"We're fine," Cap said. "Thank you."

The lady made a *hmph* noise and walked away.

I kept my hands over my breasts as I tried on the next bra, which fit okay. At least it wasn't as bad as the others.

"Okay, this one," I said. It was a 32B.

Cap read the tag: "Nice'n'Spicy."

She kissed my forehead. I screwed up my face. "This is so humiliating. Is this a big size? Are my boobs really enormous like Vicki said?"

"No, sweetheart, you just skipped the training bra."

Cap picked out one beige, one yellow, and one white bra. When we reached the counter, the woman who almost saw my breasts smiled at me as if she were the school nurse. I tried not to frown at her as she folded up my new bras.

Then she said to Cap, "I guess her parents left it to the babysitter to take her on this shopping trip."

Cap stopped writing her check in the middle of her signature. "This is my daughter," she said, staring at the lady.

"But—" the saleswoman began, "I just assumed—"

"You assumed wrong," Cap said with a hard tone she rarely used.

"An honest mistake," the woman said, shaking her head.

"A presumptuous error," Cap said.

The saleswoman didn't say another word. She handed over the bag in exchange for Cap's check.

Walking to the car, I realized I had to wear a bra for the rest of my life. Ugh.

"Can you believe what she said?" Cap asked, unlocking my door. "That white woman asked if I was babysitting you."

"Anybody can see I'm your daughter."

"Anybody who can see past skin color."

"We're practically twins—I have your feet and hands and toes and fingers," I said.

Cap walked around the car and got in. As she put the key in the ignition, she said, "You're right. We do have identical hands and feet. But you know, you and your sister may not look exactly like me, but we certainly don't look unrelated. I almost changed my mind and told her to forget the sale, but I didn't want you to have to try on all those bras again at another store."

"Thank you, Cap." I gave an exaggerated sigh of relief.

"You're welcome, honey. If those turn out not to feel right, we'll find you some that do."

I thought of Robert Cleary.

"You know what?"

"What, honey?"

"A couple of weeks ago, a boy at school said he heard my mother's black."

"He did?" She put the car in reverse, but didn't back up.

"I said you are black, but he asked like he was accusing me of something. It made me feel like the whole world's talking about me behind my back. And then a girl wanted me to eat lunch with her right after she asked if you were black, like that was the reason she wanted to be friends. A black girl."

Cap reached over and took my hand. "No matter what anyone says, Veronica, just remember that some people think black people and white people shouldn't be married."

"But you and Daddy, you're like the lovingest parents in the world."

"Yes, and we have two beautiful children together." She rubbed my arm. "But that doesn't change the way a lot of people think. Okay?"

I nodded.

As she backed out of the parking space, she asked, "So how do you feel about getting your first bra?"

"I don't like it at all. It's not comfortable."

"Oh, honey, you said this one was okay—should we go back?"

"No, I don't mean it's not comfortable. It was the least painful, but I still don't like it."

"You'll get used to it."

I had no choice. I would make these bras fit me comfortably, and I would wear them until they were shredded rags that had to be pinned closed in the back. I wasn't going through that humiliation again anytime soon.

Chapter 2

During a blizzard on the Saturday before Christmas break, Katie and I were playing in her bedroom when her eight-year-old sister Allison burst in.

"There's a black girl here with her grandmother, and she wants Mom to do her hair!"

"Get out, Allison!" Katie yelled, not looking up.

"Mom said to come and get you because this girl's in your class. I'm telling Mom you yelled at me!" Allison slammed the door.

"Who do you think it is?" Katie walked to the door, opened it slightly, and walked out.

Why had Allison gone running and blabbing through the house just because a black person had come for a haircut? Had Katie's mother never cut a black person's hair?

When Katie quietly stepped back into her room, I asked, "Who is it?"

She closed the door. "It's Maria Richardson."

My skin prickled with goosebumps. "Should we go say hi?"

"No way, she's mean. Anyway, I didn't know my mom did black peoples' hair." Katie rearranged her Scrabble squares.

I stared at my letters, knowing the best I could come up with would be a three-letter, three-point word unless Katie put out something good.

Did Katie's mother know about hot combs and Ultra Sheen? Shouldn't we at least go say hi to Maria? Wouldn't she be nice to us in front of her grandmother and Katie's mother? Or would she call Katie a "white-ass" again?

"Promise not to cheat," I said and left the room.

I walked down the hallway and peeked into the kitchen. I saw the back of a black woman sitting in the center of the tiled kitchen with pink curlers in her gray-streaked hair. Katie's mother pulled a regular comb though the woman's hair. I didn't smell heated hair, and I didn't see a hot comb on the stove.

When I walked to the living room without being noticed, I heard the TV and Allison's voice. I took a deep breath and stepped around the corner into the living room.

Both Maria and Allison looked up at me.

"Maria, are you going to get your hair done, too?" I hadn't talked to her since the day in the lunchroom.

She shook her head. She seemed so untough sitting there.

"Well, if you want, you can come and play with Katie and me—if you want." My heart pounded from my chest up to my throat. I had no idea what she would do or say in Katie's room—or even what Katie would do or say.

"All right," she said, jumping off the couch, smiling at me a little.

When we walked into the bedroom, I saw the corner of Katie's mouth turn up in a snarl. After a split second, her face relaxed and she said, "Oh, hi, Maria, we'll start a new game if you want to play, too."

We folded up the card table and put the Scrabble board on the floor. We played one game, not talking much, until none of us could come up with another word. "I have it," Katie yelled, then she spelled WART, and won the game.

"Have either of you ever had a wart?" I asked.

"I did once on my heel," Maria said, pulling off her left shoe. "I had to go to the foot doctor and he burned it off with a laser. You can see where it was. See the hole? See, right there." She pointed to a dark spot.

"Gross," Katie said. "Didn't that hurt?"

"Not really," Maria said, shrugging her shoulders, and pulling her sock and shoe back on. "But I limped so much I didn't have to go to school for a week."

"I have an idea," I said. "Let's play another game where the only words we can spell have to do with gross things like warts and pus."

"That's totally babyish, Veronica," Katie said.

"No, come on," Maria said. "It sounds fun."

"Yeah," I said. "We can each use double the letters and two holders apiece."

By the time we'd spelled out all the disgusting words we could think of, including pimple, semen, boob, tit, and dick, we were laughing and rolling around on the floor.

A knock on the door interrupted our hysteria. Maria had to go. Mrs. Simmons was done with Maria's grandmother, and she was wrapping her freshly styled silver and black hair with a plastic head cover.

Katie and I followed Maria out and said goodbye as we watched them put on heavy coats, then dash out to their car.

Back in Katie's room, she said, "For some reason, I always thought Maria was mean."

I still didn't tell Katie that Maria had called her a "white-ass."

I looked forward to seeing Maria on Monday, but I didn't see her again until Friday, the last day of school before our two-week winter vacation. She smiled at me in the lunch line and I opened my mouth to invite her to sit with us, but Maggie appeared at my side with a slice of pizza and a milk. She was wearing a super low-cut sweater, and I wanted to ask her what she was advertising.

But I was more concerned about Maria's response. She looked Maggie up and down and then rolled her eyes and walked away.

"See you later," I called after her.

She turned and smiled, but kept walking.

Chapter 3

AFTER WINTER BREAK, Mrs. Green rearranged the seating chart for English class. I now sat in front of Jude Carver, who had skin the color of walnut shells and dark brown curly hair. That made me think he was black. Then I heard another black boy make a comment that made me wonder.

"Yeah, man, but your mom's white—she wouldn't even think of whipping you with a switch."

The boy sitting in front of me, Damon, was talking to Jude. Mrs. Green cleared her throat at the front of the room. Damon turned around to face the front, but I couldn't concentrate. Was Jude's mother really white? Jude had real curls, not frizzy stuff like mine.

"We're having a quiz on Friday," Mrs. Green said as she handed out our vocabulary list. I wasn't paying attention to her; all I could do was plan how to get a good look at Jude when I turned around to hand him the vocab lists.

In the second it took to turn and reach my hand with the papers toward him, I had an imaginary conversation with him. I'd say, *Your mother's white? Mine's black.* Then Jude would say, *That's cool.*

Instead, when I handed him the papers, I just smiled at him and set them on his desk. He smiled back, and I turned around quickly.

I regretted wearing my hair down. I hadn't worn anything but a braid since Maggie's mean comment.

I was sure Jude was staring at my hair, which felt heavy like a wool afghan resting on my shoulders. My back itched where my hair was pressed between my blouse and the back of the seat. I wondered if it looked as fuzzy and wild as I imagined.

When class ended, I grabbed my things and stood up. Before I stepped away though, Jude said, "Bye, Veronica."

All I could do was smile and keep walking.

Chapter 4

JUDE WAS SO CUTE with those big brown eyes. When I saw him later in gym, he looked cuter. His skin was smooth and warm like honey. He looked mixed. I looked white. I wondered what I'd be like if my skin were the color of his. Why was Jude darker than me if we both had one black and one white parent? I was lost in my thoughts.

By the end of gym class, I had made up a theory that when a black man and white woman had a baby, the baby came out with darker skin than when a white man and a black woman had a baby—skin color must be more closely related to the father. Why, then, if I looked so white, were Jude's curls so perfect and my hair so in need of a hot comb?

Last hour of the day I had a cooking elective. When the bell rang, I discovered that I knew no one in the class. As I sat alone at a table for four, I decided that this was the worst thing ever.

I forced myself to smile at anyone who looked my way, but I felt desperate and pathetic as everyone passed me by to sit with their friends.

Class started with me alone at my table. Did I have the plague or something? Was it my giant hair? Did everybody think my hair would get in the food we were going to cook, so they didn't want me in their group?

When the teacher made up teams for cooking, I was put with three black girls. I had seen them around school, but had never spoken with any of them. They'd gone to elementary school together and seemed like best friends. We gathered in our assigned kitchen and I introduced myself.

They were Jackie, Tunisia, and Leslie. They were all taller than me, and it turned out that Jackie and Leslie were cousins. Tunisia's skin was caramel colored, and her long forehead and neck made her as exotic-looking as her name.

Mrs. Robbins, the teacher said, "I'd like you all to take a few minutes to introduce yourselves right now and also start thinking of a dish you'd like to prepare later in the quarter when you get a free cooking day. It can't be anything pre-packaged from the store. If you want to bake a cake, that's fine, but you've got to bake it from scratch. Spend the next five or six minutes thinking of some ideas."

"How about some good ol' chitlins," Leslie said.

The three of them laughed.

I smiled and looked at the floor, hesitant about joining them.

"They're good to eat, but nasty to make," Tunisia said. "My aunt can *make* some chitlins."

"How do you think Mrs. Robbins would feel if we made the whole room smell like chitlins?" Jackie said.

They all looked at me as if they'd just remembered I was part of the group.

Jackie said, "Oh, sorry—Veronica, right?"

I nodded.

"Y'all, we should include Veronica, too."

"Maybe we should make an apple pie," Tunisia said. They all laughed again.

Seriously, I thought. *They are making fun of me?* I forced myself to hold back the tears welling in my eyes. I had to let them know I couldn't be so easily insulted.

I said, "Do you know that chitlins are intestines?"

They turned up their noses and shook their heads. "We try to un-know that," Jackie said.

"They taste better when you don't think about *what* they are," Leslie said.

None of us said anything. We stood in a circle just staring at each other until I said, "Why don't we make greens?"

31

"Greens?" they all said in unison.

Then Leslie said, "This girl knows about chit-lins *and* greens? *Hmph.* What do you know about greens? Greens is soul food."

"My family eats greens," I said. "My father grows greens in his garden."

"No offense, Veronica," Leslie said, "but greens is black folks' food. I have never heard of white people eating greens before."

"I'm mixed," I said to stop them from staring at me. I was burning up in my sweater. I had an urge to chop off all my hair.

"You're what?" Leslie asked.

"My mother is black," I said.

"Your dad must be *real* white then." Tunisia laughed, then stopped when the others didn't join her. "No, I'm sorry—I wasn't laughing at you."

"Girl, yes you were," Leslie said.

I shrugged and shook my head, only able to get half my mouth into a smile. I imagined my reflection as they stared at me. Big blue eyes, white freckled skin, a mass of brown hair.

"I can tell," Leslie said.

"Girl, you're lying," Jackie said, pushing her shoulder.

"No, I can," Leslie said. "Look at that hair."

Mrs. Robbins walked up with a clipboard and asked if we'd come up with any ideas for the free cooking day.

"Greens," I said.

"Greens?" she repeated. She took her reading glasses off her nose and let them fall to her chest, dangling on the silver chain around her neck.

"It's a dish black people eat," I said. "Collard greens doctored up with about a pound of salt and a big juicy ham hock."

"Yes, I know what greens are," she said. She put her glasses back on her nose and peered at me through them. "I'm just a little surprised that you all agreed so quickly. You don't have to commit to it now. I'll have a sign-up sheet later in the week."

When Mrs. Robbins walked away, Leslie, Tunisia, and Jackie all burst out laughing. Jackie said, "Did you see the look on her face?"

"She didn't know what to think," Tunisia said.

"You must trick people all the time, huh, Veronica?"

I laughed with them. I wanted to tell them I'd never tricked anybody in my life, but stayed quiet. I didn't want to spend the next five months worrying about whether they liked me.

I hated making fun of the teacher, but at least I didn't feel like the outsider to these three girls anymore.

Chapter 5

A FEW WEEKS LATER, when the Valentine's Day dance was announced, I tried to ignore chatter in the halls and the signs on the walls. All of my friends wanted to get asked; I didn't think anybody would ask me.

Billy Williams, with his perfect teeth and feathered, sand-colored hair, asked Katie—he just walked up to her at her locker and asked, and she said yes.

A few days later, after a vocabulary quiz in English, as I handed Jude Carver the list of the next week's words, he asked if I was going to the dance.

I turned all the way around in my seat to make sure he was talking to me.

"Uhn't uh," I said.

"Would you go with me if I asked?"

I thought he was just inquiring. It never occurred to me that he'd ask me.

"Yes," I said.

I heard Mrs. Green clearing her throat. I turned around to face the front, my heart beating everywhere in my body. Jude asked me! My insides shook, and I felt like my whole body floated high above my desk.

After class, Jude said he'd see me later the way he did every day, then he touched me on the shoulder for the first time. Something squeezed my heart, and I felt hungry. I put my fingers on my neck every few minutes and felt my racing pulse when I was near him. Could everyone see and hear my heart pounding and pounding and pounding? I wondered. No boy had ever liked me before.

A week before the dance, like every other day, Jude ate lunch with his friends and I with mine. Katie and Billy didn't eat together, so I figured it was okay to eat separately. As I finished my peanut butter sandwich, Katie nudged me and said, "Here comes Jude."

I looked up. Jude was walking towards me between rows of tables, his hands stuffed into his pockets, his eyes on the ground.

"He looks sad," Katie said.

I began sucking furiously on the peanut butter coating the roof of my mouth. I couldn't talk. I reached for my milk, but it was empty. I grabbed my throat, massaging it to help the peanut butter go down.

Katie shoved her milk in my face and I took a huge swallow just as Jude said my name. I swallowed air again, my heart hammered. My eyes watered.

"Can we talk?" Jude said, his eyes drooping. "In private," he whispered.

I felt the eyes of everyone at my table on us. I grabbed my apple and crumpled my brown bag.

As we walked out of the cafeteria to the hallway, I knew everyone was looking at us. Not just my friends, but people we didn't know and who didn't know us.

"You look like something's wrong," I said.

"I broke a window playing baseball on Saturday," he said, his hands still in his pockets.

"You play baseball in the winter?"

"Yeah, in the snow, just for fun. Except, not for fun this time—got grounded."

"Oh no…"

"You're gonna hate me, but I begged and begged, and my mom still says I can't go to the dance. I even told her how disappointed you'd be. She's a girl, she should understand stuff like that."

"Oh, it's okay," I said, lying. I felt sweat trickling in my underarms.

"You're not mad?"

"Nope." I shifted my weight from foot to foot as I stared into his big brown eyes.

"You don't hate me?"

"Mmn't mmm." I shook my head then bit into my apple.

"Aww, I thought you'd hate me. You'll still talk to me in Mrs. Green's class?"

"Of course." I hoped he was being sincere about being in trouble.

I cried in bed that night.

Vicki went to parties all the time. She hung out with boys and played kiss-in-the-closet games. I knew because I heard her talking about boys all the time to her best friend Lana.

Why was it so impossible for me to go to a dance with a boy? I wish Jude hadn't asked me in the first place. Then it would be normal not to be going.

Jude was so cute, and I felt comfortable around him, and I liked him a lot. He made me laugh, and he whispered things to the back of my neck when he knew Mrs. Green wasn't watching.

The next day I wanted to cry again when I walked into Mrs. Green's room and saw Jude talking to a girl who sat on the other side of the room. I sat in my seat without looking at him and pulled out my homework. I started re-reading it, not remembering one sentence to the next.

I wanted Jude behind me, even though the bell hadn't rung yet. He dumped me, then deserted me.

What if he asked Mrs. Green if he could sit on the other side of the room for good? What if he'd made up the winter baseball story so he could be free to ask that other girl to the dance?

When the bell rang, I watched him approach out of the corner of my eye. He slugged me softly in the shoulder as he walked past me.

"Hey, Veronica," he said. "Why are you studying so hard? We don't have a quiz until Friday."

"I know." I smiled, but my heart still ached, convinced that he didn't want to go to the dance with me, broken window or not.

Chapter 6

Two days before the dance during gym class, as we ran around playing hockey on the freshly polished floor, a boy with dark hair and bright blue eyes named Kevin Vogel picked me to be on his team. He was always a captain, no matter what sport we played, and he'd never picked me before.

During the first game, I scored three goals, my record, and I played great because I didn't want to let Kevin down.

During the second game, I played goalie for my team, and Kevin came and talked to me while everybody else stood in the center waiting for the puck to be dropped.

"You're playing great," he said, patting me on the back.

"Thanks for picking me," I said.

"I had to find a way to ask you to the dance," he said.

I felt myself blush. "The Valentine's Day dance?"

"Do you know of some other dance?"

"KEVIN!" someone shouted from the center of the gym.

My mind was racing. Two boys asking me to the dance? Was I lucky Jude broke that window?

"Well?"

"Okay," I said, leaning my chin on the end of my hockey stick.

"KEVIN!"

"I gotta go," he said, turning and walking backwards away from me.

I curled my top lip under and bit it to keep my face from exploding into a smile. When we started playing again, I let nearly every puck the other team shot into the goal. Kevin replaced me with somebody else, but he winked at me when he did it, so I didn't mind.

As I walked to my new position on the offense, he whispered, "I bet you're a better dancer."

That night during dinner I told Cap, Daddy, and Vicki that I was going to the dance with a boy with dark brown hair and blue eyes.

"Oh," Cap said excitedly. "Did he go to Einstein with you?"

"No," I said. I wasn't sure which elementary school Kevin had attended.

"She was going with another boy," Vicki said.

"Oh, you're really popular, Veronica," Cap said with a smile.

"The first boy's mother's white and his father's black, right, Veronica?" Vicki asked.

"I should've told you before, about Jude," I said, feeling ashamed for not telling Cap and Daddy about Jude at the time. I still liked Jude. He still flipped my braid to get my attention in English, but it had been so painful when he canceled our date. Besides, how does Vicki know that when she's not even at the same school?

"But you're telling us now," Cap said.

"Why aren't you going with Jude?" Daddy asked with a concerned look.

"He broke a window playing baseball," I said.

Vicki shook her head. "Yeah, right. In February?"

"He said he plays in the snow." I didn't want her to be right, and I felt bad for wondering the same thing. "Anyway, I'm going with Kevin now."

Daddy said, "Congratulations, Veronica. Your first date."

"Daddy! It's not a date till somebody drives, right, Vicki?"

"Yup," she said, smiling. "That's the rule of thumb."

I still felt embarrassed about all this talk about boys with my parents.

Chapter 7

THE AFTERNOON OF THE dance, I overheard Vicki on the phone with Lana. From what I'd heard Vicki say so far, I figured out that Lana had been at the mall on Friday night and some kids from school had gotten in a fight.

"I don't think I know him," Vicki said.

I wrote "Who?" on a piece of paper and set it on the table before her.

She crumpled the paper and shooed me away with her hand.

"He said that?" she said, her eyes opening wider.

"Who?" I mouthed.

"Go away!" she said. "Go on, Lana."

I needed her help picking out something to wear. I went back to my room and looked in my closet. At that moment, I hated all my clothes, from my brown corduroys to my frilly Easter dress.

I could wear the outfit I wore for the choir concert in seventh grade. But it was plain and ugly and boring. Besides, I was sure my friends would remember. I pulled out a dark blue dress with big, bright flowers all over it. I could wear blue tights and my red shoes since some of the flowers were red. They'd look like red dancing shoes, I thought, smiling about my choice.

My stomach gurgled. Dinner was in an hour. Then I would get dressed and Cap would drop me off at school where I'd meet Kevin. I went back into the dining room and watched Vicki talk on the phone.

"...wouldn't do that. He's in my homeroom," she said. "Okay, Lana, bye."

"Why'd you hang up so quickly?" I asked.

"Her sister had to use the phone. Why is that any of your business?" she said, standing to hang up the phone in the kitchen.

"What were you talking about?" I followed her.

"Why do you need to know?"

"It sounded important. I think I should know."

"Some boys from school got in a fight at the mall last night. Are you satisfied?"

"Who were they?"

"I doubt you know them."

"What are their names?"

"Leave me alone now, pesky little girl." She walked into her bedroom and shut the door in my face.

"Vicki, you have to help me pick out an outfit for tonight." I pounded my fist on the door. "I don't want to look dumb."

She opened the door and rolled her eyes. "Can't you just figure it out by yourself? Nobody showed me all the stuff to do, you know."

She walked into my room and pointed to the dress I'd picked out. "Are you going to wear *that?*"

"Yes, why, do you think it's ugly?"

"Are you wearing the red shoes so you'll look like Dorothy in the *Wizard of Oz?* If you're having a bad time, you can click your heels together and say, 'There's no place like home.'"

She grabbed the shoes and hit the heels together.

"Quit! Those are my good red shoes. Give them back!" I tried grabbing them, but she held them up above her head. I climbed on the bed but she walked to the center of the room. "Vicki!" I yelled, then, "Da-addy!"

"Victoria!" Daddy called sternly from the living room.

She handed me the shoes. "Don't you have any blue shoes? Or black? The red ones are way too loud. I like the dress, but not the red shoes."

At dinner, Cap told us that on Friday night she drove past the mall and saw two police cars speeding through the parking lot. "On the news last night, they said some sort of fight broke out inside and one boy really got hurt. A white boy."

"Yeah," Vicki said. "Lana said a boy in eleventh grade, a white kid, was yelling some nasty things at some black kids from the high school. I guess he thought he could get away with it."

"Do you know any of the boys?" Daddy asked.

"They're in Lana's older sister's grade. She said they had to go to the police station and get booked or something."

"And the white boy?" Cap asked.

"His name is Marc Vogel…" Vicki said, casually.

I started choking. The half-chewed meatloaf in my mouth had gone down the wrong pipe. I held my napkin in front of my mouth as I coughed.

"Hands above your head," Daddy said, raising his own as an example.

I raised my arms and the coughing stopped. I drank two huge gulps of water. No one ate while I caught my breath. I was burning up.

"Okay," I said, "I'm okay now."

"What did you say his name was, Vicki?" Cap asked.

I held my breath as she repeated the name. I wasn't going to choke again.

"Marc Vogel," she said. "Lana's sister said he said some really—oh, my God, horrible things, and the other kids just beat him up. They may have even broken some bones."

"Oh, no," Cap said. "Was it because he's white and they're black?"

Vicki nodded, bobbing her head up and down.

In less than two hours I would be dancing with the second boy who ever asked me to a dance. Not only that, but this boy's brother might be in the hospital because he'd been beaten up for saying bad things to some black kids.

What was I going to do? I couldn't let Cap and Daddy know that my Kevin was related to that boy from the mall fight.

I didn't look up at them; I just took a few small bites of corn on the cob. I didn't want to go to the dance. What was I supposed to do now that I knew Kevin's brother was a racist?

Vicki repeated some of what Marc had said. I tried not to listen. I hated Marc for being related to Kevin. How could anyone be so awful and mean? Had the other boys at the mall made him angry enough to say those things?

"Veronica," Daddy whispered, "You've hardly touched your food."

"I'm not hungry." I stared at my cold meatloaf.

"You're going to need lots of energy later for the dance."

"Maybe I'll have some food there. Vicki, do they have food at dances?"

"There's always punch and snacks." She started talking about the fight again.

I moved my green beans around on my plate for a minute, then asked to be excused.

On my bed, I almost started crying. I was so worried about Kevin and his family and what they would think when they found out Cap was black.

I couldn't stand to think about it anymore, so I got dressed. As I tried to manage my hair, the sight of myself in the mirror, the white skin, the pink-orange freckles, blue eyes—the only reflection I'd ever known—reminded me that Kevin had no reason to think anything was different about me. Kevin probably assumed like everybody else that I was just another white girl.

Without looking in the mirror, I parted my hair down the middle and braided it down my back.

I walked into Vicki's room wearing all blue: dress, tights and shoes. I'd even ironed the collar of the dress so it would stay in place. While I ironed it,

I zoned out, trying to figure out how to tell Kevin I was not, in fact, just another white girl.

I kept misting spray starch on it—too much. The top of the dress fit tightly across my chest, but the stiff white collar with its red bow in the center hung down to cover it, so I hoped nobody would notice.

"Your hair looks horrible," Vicki said. "Did you forget to do it on purpose? Come here. I'll fix it."

"Can you make a ponytail on the side with a braid? Please make all of my hair smooth and flat. Maybe you should put some of Cap's VO5 on it."

"Here, sit down."

As she unbraided my hair and began brushing it all to one side, she said, "So, aren't you going to ask more about that fight at the mall?"

"I don't want to know any more," I said.

"But before you wouldn't leave me alone about it," she said.

"I've heard enough. I don't care about mall fights."

"Fine," she said. "So, are you nervous about the dance?"

"No," I said quickly. I couldn't tell Vicki I felt nervous about my date being related to that horrible boy from the mall fight. I was surprised she didn't know my *not-date* Kevin was the brother of the mall fight kid.

"That's good. You'll have a better time if you're not sick to your stomach with worry."

She made my hair smooth and flat on top and poufy in the braid, which hung at the perfect level on the left side of my head, just a few inches above my ear. I thanked her and walked into the living room where Daddy sat with the camera. He took pictures of me as I walked toward the piano. I made funny faces because I felt silly about being the only one in the room all dressed up.

"Kev-vin," Vicki kept calling from her room, around the corner. "Oh, Kev-vin, my dar-ling, Kev-vin!"

"Quit teasing me!" I yelled, tears welling in my eyes.

Cap appeared with her makeup bag. Daddy snapped more pictures while Cap brushed her blush onto my cheeks.

"Now you look grown up," she said. "Here, sweetheart," she held out a pink and white tube. "My lipstick is not the right color for you, so I picked this up from the drugstore today."

The label read *Hint of Pink*. "I thought we couldn't wear makeup until we were in high school?"

"This doesn't really count as makeup. It's like ChapStick," she said, kissing me on the forehead.

"Pink ChapStick," Daddy said, taking a picture of Cap kissing my forehead.

I'd never felt so grown up in front of my parents before. Vicki had just this year started wearing makeup. I put my new lipstick in my black purse with some tissues, four one dollar bills, a couple of dimes, two quarters, and the penny I'd found in the driveway that morning. Also in my purse I had a pen and a pad of paper, my house keys, and an old double-mirrored compact of Cap's.

I kissed Daddy good-bye on the cheek. I felt the gooey lip gloss rub off and I laughed. "Sorry, I got your cheek all gross."

"That's okay," he said. He hugged me tightly. "You look beautiful tonight, Veronica. I hope you have a wonderful time."

"Are you ready, Veronica?" Cap jingled her car keys.

"Uh-huh."

Vicki walked into the room. "Your hair has never looked better. My compliments to your stylist."

"*Thanks*, Vicki."

Chapter 8

A T THE CURB OF Pepper Junior High, I kissed Cap good-bye in the car and told her I'd see her at ten o'clock out front when the dance was over.

"Make sure he behaves," she said, twisting the curl at the end of my braid around her index finger.

"Okay." I scanned Pepper's big front porch, but didn't see Kevin. I saw Katie and Billy standing by the door and knew they were waiting for me. "There's Katie. Bye, Cap," I said, kissing her again, feeling the last of the pink lipstick come off my lips.

"When can I meet him?" she asked as I leaned in to grab my purse.

"I don't see him yet." I felt a tightening inside my body, fearing suddenly she'd ask me his last name and then she'd know that he was related to the boy from the mall fight.

"How about when you pick me up?" *Maybe by then*, I thought, *I will have told him about Cap being black.*

"Have a good time, honey, I love you."

"I love you, too," I said, stepping back onto the curb.

I watched her drive away. During the few minutes we drove to school, I'd forgotten about Marc Vogel. Now all of a sudden I could think of nothing else.

Suddenly, as I walked across the huge porch toward Katie and Billy, I felt a bit of relief: *Maybe Kevin won't show up!*

"Veronica!"

I turned to see Kevin walking toward me. His hair looked clean and brushed, something I'd never seen before. He was wearing khaki pants and a light blue oxford with a tie with red and dark blue flowers. As he walked under the lights of the porch roof, I realized the red and blue matched my dress. We couldn't have planned our outfits better than this. Vicki would think I was childish for even thinking that, so I kept it to myself.

"Hi, Kevin."

We walked toward each other. He grabbed my hand and we headed for Katie and Billy, who were staring at us.

My hand sweat *so* much in Kevin's that I feared it would slide out of his. My heart pounded so hard in my throat and my chest, I thought it might explode. If I started laughing, I'd have a seizure like I saw a boy do during the summer once at the Maple Hills pool. I was a mess of emotions!

I couldn't wait to be inside the dark gym where the lights would be dim and we could dance. I wasn't sure at what point I'd ask Kevin about his brother, or if I would at all. Maybe I could get through this night and never speak to him again.

"We have to freshen up," Katie said as soon as we were inside the building.

She pulled my hand hard in the direction of the bathroom.

"I hate this bathroom. It always stinks like smoke," I said.

"I have to pee." Katie pushed open the door. "Anyway, listen: Billy and I were making out before you came."

I gasped. "*Making out?*"

"He kissed me and he was trying to touch my boobs!" She walked into the stall on the end.

"I hope Kevin doesn't do that. I wouldn't have any idea what to do if he did," I said, smoothing the top of my hair in my reflection. I opened my purse and pulled out my pink lipstick. I applied one coat, then another, then I circled my whole mouth with it.

"Just go along with it," Katie said. "That's what Maggie McDougall told me to do."

"Maggie McDougall said so? If I were you, I'd do the exact opposite of whatever *she* says to do." I wiped off the excess lipstick with a paper towel.

"How come?"

"My sister said Maggie McDougall wears a red bathing suit to the pool because she knows it'll be see-through when it gets wet. Everybody knows that about red bathing suits."

Katie flushed the toilet and washed her hands. "I think she got a new bathing suit at the end of the summer."

"I'm sure it's a white one—they're see-through, too."

"That's mean," Katie said. "Anyway, I'll tell you if Billy tries anything Maggie warned me about."

"I don't want to know about whatever Maggie warned you about."

We smiled as we walked up to our dates. I felt myself grow red and hot all over as the bathroom conversation with Katie ran through my head.

We followed the sound of a loud bass beat to the gym. I took a deep breath when I saw how the gym had been transformed with Valentine's Day colors—pink and red and white. Heart-shaped balloons were tied in groups of four or five every ten feet around the edge of the floor that we scuffed every day playing hockey and basketball and dodge ball. The lights were low, but the glossy shine was coming off the floor. I was glad to discover that one of the walls was lined with tables of food and drinks, because if the butterflies ever settled in my stomach, I'd be hungry.

Kevin pulled me aside and said, "You look really nice tonight. I wanted to bring you something special, so I got this." From his pocket, he pulled a yellow rosebud with a stem about two inches long. The petals were warm and wilted from being inside his jacket pocket. When he turned around, I put the rosebud in my purse. Where else was I going to put it?

"Are you hungry?" Kevin helped himself to the snacks on a table just inside the door.

I shook my head, still too nervous to eat, but I watched him shove fistfuls of snack mix into his mouth. He smacked his hands together and said, "Come on. Let's go boogie."

He grabbed my hand and pulled me through the crowd. Before we stopped walking, a slow Marvin Gaye song started playing. Kevin turned toward me with his arms stretched out. I hoped he wasn't planning on doing the tango or anything silly. I didn't know what else to do, so I walked into his arms and put my arms around him. He closed his arms around my back.

For a few seconds I floated, letting the music flow into my head. Up close, Kevin smelled like Ivory soap and Doritos, a good combination for him. I felt his hand on my back, at the bottom of my spine. My right hand was somewhere in the middle of his back, resting sort of heavily in the spot where it landed. My other hand hung awkwardly so I raised it, careful not to touch Kevin's back with my sweaty palm, and put it around his neck. I closed my eyes and felt the music beating through me.

We rocked on the sides of our feet back and forth, again and again. I felt so, so, so, so very good I didn't want the song to end. Dancing with Kevin was like being in a continual hug. His hand on the bottom of my back was making little circles. I was scared to move my head back at all—that would put our faces close enough for him to kiss me.

I'd never been kissed before. I let my neck relax and my head droop on his shoulder. I was the perfect height for him.

The song ended, and the band picked up the melody a little longer, but I knew it would end and a fast song would start.

A loud, pulsing disco song began. We pulled ourselves apart and shook our butts and flailed our arms and moved our feet for a while, smiling at each other the whole time, then we headed back to the punch and chips.

The singer of the band said, "We're taking a break, but we'll put on some CD's so you can keep dancing if you want. We'll be right back."

I drank a cup of punch and realized I needed to go to the bathroom soon. Kevin saw a cluster of his friends walking out of the gym and said he'd stay with them until I got back.

Out in the hallway, I headed for the bathroom. "Yo, Veronica…"

I recognized my cousin James's deep voice and turned to see his beaming smile. His mother, Aunt Glenda, was Cap's sister. She and Uncle Desmond and James and his brother, Franklin, lived in the all-black township where kids were picked up and bussed to our school and others in better school districts. James was a senior in high school, and Franklin had graduated a few years earlier. Both were musicians.

"Hi, James," I said.

"Hey, Veronica." James leaned down and gave me a hug. "My mom said you'd be here tonight. Don't you look so dressed up, too? Hey, girl, where's your date?"

"He's—it's not a date. No car. I got dropped off," I laughed, trying to avoid the topic of Kevin. James knew everyone at the high school, no doubt including Kevin's brother.

"So your non-date, then. He's what?" James pulled his drumsticks out of his back pocket and began tapping the air between us, something he always did.

"In the bathroom, I think," I said. "Or getting some punch. Maybe he's dancing."

"Date or no date, sounds like you need to keep an eye on him, V."

"I know." I laughed, a cramp stabbing me in my gut. *Great, is this my period coming now out of the blue?* I grimaced as I tried to keep smiling at James. I couldn't tell James or my family about my date until I found out the truth about Kevin's brother from Kevin himself.

"Well, I gotta get back to work. Bring him over and introduce him to me later. I'll be on the stage behind the drum set."

"I will," I lied.

He flashed a smile, spreading his arms and drumsticks out like bird's wings.

He beat the air. "Drum roll!" he called as he disappeared down the hallway.

I made my way to the bathroom where I found Kevin standing outside the door waiting for me.

"Veronica. I thought you were inside already. Katie went looking for you. Where'd you go?"

"I took the long way."

He laughed, and I stared into his pink mouth. How was I going to introduce Kevin to James?

"You know what?" he said. "I could've sworn that black guy with the drumsticks was checking you out."

I laughed at first because he must've meant James and he was my cousin, but then I realized I couldn't simply tell Kevin that. "Don't be silly."

What's happening to me? I thought. *I'm lying to my cousin. I'm standing here with Kevin denying I was talking to said cousin, who is one of the coolest and nicest dudes in the world. Just say it: Kevin, I'm black!*

I felt sort of numb. I said nothing.

Kevin continued. "No, I mean it. You better watch out." He leaned close to me and I felt his warm breath on my cheek. "My parents always tell my sister that black boys are trouble. She's in eleventh grade. My dad caught her sneaking out with one once, and he beat the crap out of her."

My mind stuck on the word "one," as if he'd been speaking of extraterrestrials.

"He beat her?" I couldn't remember the last time I'd gotten a spanking.

"Yeah, with a belt. It was sick. She screamed and screamed and screamed. She hasn't done it again, so I guess it worked." Kevin stopped at a table with big bowls of chips and Doritos on it. He grabbed a handful and began munching. "Are you hungry?"

Now the smell was making me nauseous. "No, not at all."

"Why do you look like that?"

"I'm thinking about what you said."

"About my dad beating my sister?"

"Yes—I don't understand what your parents think is wrong with black kids."

"No, not just black kids, all black people. 'They're trouble, with a capital T,' my dad says. He says they're the reason our neighborhood is getting so bad. They drive down the price of our house, he says."

"So your father thinks black people are bad and you shouldn't talk to them because…why?"

"That's not what I mean. You can *talk* to them, but you shouldn't let your parents know, that's all. I have a few black friends, but I never invite them over or tell my parents if I—"

"I have to go," I said. "Don't wait for me." I ran out, back to the bathroom. I pushed open the door, and scanned the room for Katie, but didn't see her.

While I waited for a stall to open up, I forgot about Kevin for a second as I watched straight-haired girls toss their hair to make it feather back. Fine hair always did that. Sometimes they'd complain about how flat their hair was and how it wouldn't hold a curl all day.

Not mine, I thought, though I wished I could have flat hair for a day. How I would love to comb through it, play with it, and toss my head around. All the girls in front of the mirror were white. The eighth grade was at least half black—where were all of the black girls?

Right here, I thought, hugging my arms around myself.

Should I go out and tell him my mother's black? I wondered. *Should I go call Cap from a pay phone and tell her I was out with the brother of the boy who'd gotten beaten up in the mall and it turns out he's a racist?*

She'd be so disappointed in me for not saying something during dinner. I could say I didn't know.

When it was my turn, I closed the stall door. I pulled out my compact, and looked at myself in it behind the privacy of the closed door. "You can't just ignore it," I said quietly. Only one eye reflected at a time in the tiny mirror, and I stared deeply into it to find the answer. I saw the big, dark pupil surrounded by the blue-gray iris centered in the white, milky eyeball. I blinked my lashes and squinted into my reflection.

Looking in my own eye, I knew what to do, but I hated how hard it was going to be.

My temples throbbed as I entered the gym. Kevin stood right where we'd been standing earlier at the punch table. He handed me a cup as soon as I reached him. I tried to recall exactly what he'd said just a few minutes earlier, but I couldn't remember specifically. I couldn't bring back the exact phrases that sounded so ridiculously stupid and racist.

Could I have heard him wrong? Or had my brain jumbled his words? I watched him munch potato chips, a handful at a time as he searched the gym, his eyes wide open. Kevin chewed with his mouth open. The crunch escaping through his lips seemed louder than the music filling the gym. He didn't have any idea that I was disgusted with him.

"Let's go find Katie and Billy," he said, setting down his cup and bowl. "And then we'll go dance some more."

I set down my punch cup. My top lip quivered. "Kevin, I think I'm going to be sick." I dashed out the doors, and through the hall to the front porch.

The cold air felt good as it stung my face, which was hot with anger.

Kevin caught up with me outside. "What's wrong?" he yelled.

"I have to know right this minute what happened to your brother at the mall last night!"

I bit down hard on my lip to stop it from twitching.

"What'd you hear?" he snapped, stuffing his hands in his pockets.

"Awful things."

"Well, you shouldn't believe everything you hear."

"Well, tell me the truth then."

He took a few deep breaths. "The truth? My brother had to go to the hospital with two broken fingers and a fractured wrist." He lowered his voice. "It's not really that bad. They checked some internal stuff, then let him go home, I guess. He's really okay."

"What did he say that made somebody break his fingers?"

"My dad told me that Marc was minding his own business when these big black kids from the high school just decided to pick on him because he's white."

"What do you mean, 'just minding his own business'? That makes no sense."

"That's how my dad explained it to me. My dad was in another store—"

"Your father was with him when he got beaten up?"

"No, they split up. We always do that when we go to the mall with our parents, don't you?"

"No," I said. The last time I'd gone to the mall with Daddy, we'd been holding hands because it had been so crowded and we didn't want to lose each other.

"Well, anyway, they split up and Marc was buying a cookie from the Cookie Factory."

"Hey, I just thought of something."

"What?" He took his hands out of his pockets and blew on them.

"Maybe it was the guys your sister got spanked for, for sneaking out with."

"My dad already thought of that. He says it doesn't matter if it was, because the only reason Marc got hit was because he's white. My dad says he's going to find out who it was and press charges."

"Press charges?"

"You know, take them to court. Get them thrown in jail. It's like my dad always says, Veronica, black guys are trouble. You ought to be glad I warned you about that guy earlier."

I burped quietly and became aware of all the punch churning in my stomach. Cherry 7-Up-flavored heartburn stuck to the back of my throat. I ran over to the edge of the big porch, the hard soles of my blue shoes scratching on the pebbles, and leaned over the railing, my hands sticking to its cold moistness, and stared into the dark bushes. Was I going to throw up?

Kevin called my name several times, high and whiny.

I spit sour mouth juice into the bush.

Suddenly, a door opened and an adult voice yelled, "What's the problem over there?" It was a chaperone, who would throw us out and call our parents if we didn't get back inside right away. We would be in big trouble for leaving the dance and loitering outside the building. I had to recover quickly.

"We better go back inside," Kevin said.

The chaperone was my homeroom teacher, Mrs. Jeffries. "Once you're inside, you've got to stay inside, kids."

I glanced at the pay phone right outside the gym but decided against calling home and asking to be picked up early. It would be easier to get through this night with Kevin than to tell Cap and Daddy the truth. Kevin was Marc Vogel's brother. I would just make it a point to keep our conversation off the subject of black people. That was all I could do for now. Besides, the dance was over in less than two hours.

Katie greeted us at the door. "Where have you two been all this time? Veronica, why is your hair all messed up?"

I reached up and smoothed my hair, pressing it down with the palm of my hand. "We were outside talking."

Billy nudged Kevin in the arm and I made a face at him.

Katie grabbed my arm and pulled me close to her. She whispered in my ear, "Were you making out?"

"Not at all. Not. At. All." I held down another sour burp. I excused myself and darted into the bathroom. I stood in the stall crying into a handful of toilet paper, the noise of excited mirror-gazers drowning out my sobs. When I finally returned, I decided to dance with Kevin only because it would pass time, but I didn't slow-dance with him because I didn't want to be that close to him.

I kept excusing myself to the bathroom, claiming the punch was making me have to go so frequently, and Kevin believed me.

When I went back inside the gym toward the end of the night after about my fifth potty break, I couldn't find Kevin anywhere. I walked around until I spotted him at the edge of the stage.

I gasped. Kevin was not five feet from my cousin James and they were talking. I started tearing through the crowd to get to them, to pull Kevin away from James, to tell him off, and maybe to punch his lights out, if I could. When I was close enough, though, James was smiling his big hearty grin. The music pumped loudly.

James handed his drumsticks down to Kevin. Kevin climbed onto the stage and positioned himself on James's little stool behind the shining silver drum set.

"Veronica!" I turned to see Katie dancing next to me.

"You've got to dance if you're on the dance floor," Billy said, lifting my arms from my sides.

How long had I stood still in the middle of a crowd of flailing bodies? I imagined seeing myself from above, like an overhead shot in a movie, where all the noise disappeared around me and only I could see what was happening while I moved in slow motion. Katie and Billy each grabbed an arm, but all the energy in my body was focused in my eyes and in my brain as I watched Kevin's grinning face as he played James's drums along with the band.

My feet felt like cement until the song finished. Kevin's hair flopped around as he did a drum roll, then shook hands with James. I watched him jump off the stage and head toward the center. He couldn't have known I was there, so I ducked toward the door and hid in the bathroom again.

When I came out he was standing right there. "Hey! Did you see me? Wasn't I awesome?"

"Kevin," I leaned close enough to smell his damp hair, "I thought you said you don't like black people."

He burst out laughing. "No, my dad says they're bad for certain things, but—did you see the way that guy played the drums? Did I tell you I play the drums? He was so cool to let me play them. I don't let anyone touch my drums!"

I felt a little like smiling because it was so clear that everything Kevin had said earlier was not really what he believed. He was just repeating what his racist father believed.

"Forget what I said about that guy giving you the eye." He put his arm around my shoulder.

"Why don't you go get his autograph?"

"What for?"

"Because you like him so much. I bet he becomes famous one day."

"He probably wouldn't give it to me."

"I bet he will."

"If we bet, you'd lose, that's for sure."

"Okay, let's bet then, if you're so sure. How about if he says yes, I get to be captain of hockey this week in gym."

Kevin shook his head, but one corner of his mouth was smiling.

"I get to pick all the team members," I said.

He laughed.

"Okay, how about if he gives you his autograph, when Mrs. Dudda tells you to pick your team on Monday, you announce to the whole gym class that you're handing over your captainship to me because you know I'd make better decisions for the team."

Kevin laughed so hard he doubled over. "And what if you lose?"

"Then… I'll bring you a bagel from the deli I pass on my way to school every morning."

"With lox and cream cheese?"

"Only if you win."

"Okay, come on," he said, pulling my hand. "This is going to be totally embarrassing, but just to prove you're wrong, I'll do it."

Halfway across the dance floor, I slipped behind a pole. I peeked around to make sure Kevin had made his way to the stage. James's face lit up when Kevin approached. This made me smile, but I didn't want to go near them. I would have to tell Kevin in my own time that I am black. Not now.

Leaning against the pole, I pretended to scan the crowd around me. Katie saw me and, still dancing, asked what I was doing.

"I lost Kevin," I lied.

"I just saw him," she said. "There he is—here he comes."

"Katie," Kevin called.

"She's right here!" Katie pulled my arm so Kevin could see me.

"What happened?" he asked.

"Did you get his autograph?"

"If I said no, how would you know I wasn't lying? You weren't there to watch."

"Oh, I—"

"I got it." He lifted up a piece of paper with my cousin's fancy signature written on it.

"What's going on?" Katie demanded.

"You're looking at the new captain of Mrs. Dudda's sixth hour gym class hockey team. Right, Kevin?"

"Right." Kevin gave me a smile that made me think he really liked me, or he wouldn't have put himself through all this.

We danced, all fast songs, until the band stopped playing and the overhead lights came on. Outside, I didn't see Cap's car yet, but Kevin spotted his sister in his family's car at the curb.

"Thanks for going with me, Veronica." He leaned forward and kissed me on the lips quickly— as fast as I kissed Cap and Daddy good-night. He walked out to the curb and opened the door of a dark-colored station wagon. He waved from inside the car as it pulled away.

Was that just my first kiss? I raised my arm and waved my hand. He'd done it so casually. I licked my lips together but couldn't taste any lip gloss. I stood for a minute trying to decide whether that kiss could be considered a real kiss. I got a little lost in my thoughts until I realized Cap was at the curb, honking to get my attention. I wiped off my lips with the back of my hand as I ran to the car.

"Were you waving at someone?" Cap asked.

"Me?"

Cap laughed. "Yes, you. Where's Kevin?" She scanned the big porch before pulling away.

"His sister just picked him up."

"Oh, too bad. I would've loved to meet him. Maybe another time. Did you have fun?"

"Yeah. James played in the band."

"Yes, Glenda told me he would be. Did you get a chance to talk to him?"

"Yeah, I did. He even let Kevin play his drums."

"Does he know?" She meant did he know she was black.

"Cap," I moaned. I hated when she asked that question, especially since Kevin didn't know and telling him was going to be difficult. I would tell him, but I couldn't just blurt it out. Cap was probably assuming I'd been with Kevin when James let him play his drums.

Cap's question went unanswered as we pulled into our driveway. I thought about the things Kevin had said during the dance. Nobody could tell, not even Kevin, just by looking at me that I was black.

I fell asleep trying to remember Kevin kissing me and trying to forget the things he had said about black people and then later half-denied. He had kissed me so quickly. He had said so casually that black people were bad. What did he mean? Would he kiss me again?

Chapter 9

Sunday morning, I awoke to the smell of bacon and pancakes. I shoved the blankets back and sat up. My blue dress draped over the back of my desk chair. Getting up meant facing my parents and answering the inevitable question of whether I had a good time with Kevin. Telling the truth and lying at the same time. I flopped back down and closed my eyes. A minute later, I opened them to see Daddy pulling back the curtains.

"Daddy," I groaned.

"Rise and shine. It's almost noon. Come tell Cap and me about last night over some breakfast."

Vicki was out with her friends. Cap served us each a plate of pancakes.

As I wolfed down my butter- and syrup-covered pancakes, I described the gym. I told them the floor had been polished so high for the dance you could almost see your reflection. I told them about the snacks on all the tables and how I saw a boy stuff his jacket pockets with pretzels and M&M's. I told them that two boys almost started punching each other over a girl in my class, and the vice principal sent the boys home. All the things I saw when I was trying to figure out Kevin.

"What about Kevin?" Cap asked.

"Does he want you to be his girlfriend?" Daddy asked.

"Daddy, that's a Vicki question!"

"Okay, let me ask it another way. Do you want to have him as your boyfriend?"

"Are you going together now? Do kids still call it going steady?"

"I don't know." I wanted to evaporate. No boy had ever liked me before, except Jude. I didn't even want to talk about it—I might jinx it.

Of course I want to be his girlfriend! I couldn't look up from my plate, afraid it was written all over my face. I moved the last bite of pancakes through the syrup.

"It's perfectly natural to like a boy," Daddy said. "You don't have to feel embarrassed, Veronica."

"I can't help it," I said, really feeling embarrassed about the stuff Kevin had said.

"Okay, sweetheart, enough about Kevin," Cap said. "Were all your friends there?"

"Katie was there, but nobody else was asked. They didn't want to go alone. I would've gone alone if Kevin hadn't asked me."

"If Kevin hadn't asked you, somebody else would've," Daddy said. "Wasn't Kevin your second choice?"

"That's right," Cap said. "Just think, by the time you get to high school, the phone will be ringing off the hook with boys trying to date you."

"I only got asked by two boys." I felt myself growing warmer. "Did I tell you James was in the band?"

"That reminds me," Cap said, "I need to call Glenda." She got up and grabbed the phone in the kitchen.

Daddy said the inquisition was over and that I could be excused. I went to my room and opened my math book. I didn't want to think about Kevin or whether he'd call, so I worked ahead on the next two chapters. Each time the phone rang, I feared it was him. I wanted to talk to him, and I wanted confirmation that he still liked me, but I also needed to think of the exact words I would use to tell him that my mother was black. I tore out a blank sheet of notebook paper and wrote out some practice statements.

Kevin, what you said about black people was hurtful because my mother is…

Kevin, if you think you're better than black people, I can't be with you.

(I reminded myself he hadn't asked me to be with him so this sentence wouldn't work.)

Kevin, I'm half black. James is my cousin. You owe us an apology.

When I went to bed that night, Kevin hadn't called all day. Still, I tossed and turned before I fell asleep, thinking of what I would say. Sometime after my clock read midnight, I decided I would give Kevin the benefit of the doubt; I wanted more than anything for him to like me. I wanted to dance with Kevin again. I wanted to walk down the halls holding hands the way some girls did. I wanted a boyfriend; I wanted him to kiss me again.

I could forgive him for saying those stupid things. Eventually, he would apologize. Once he met my family and maybe even James's family, he'd know that black people were no different from white people. I was sure it would all work out fine in the end.

I walked to school the next day full of energy though I'd hardly slept at all. I was excited to find Kevin on the big porch before school. I hadn't talked to Katie on Sunday because she'd been with her father and his new wife, but I was almost positive she wasn't worried about Billy or whether he liked her. They'd made out so they were officially going steady, even if he hadn't exactly asked her. Even if nobody uses those words anymore.

As I bought my morning bagel at Hammerstein's Deli, I remembered the bet. Losing would mean buying Kevin a bagel with lox and cream cheese for a week.

"Anything else?" the man behind the counter asked.

"I'd also like a plain bagel with lox and cream cheese." I couldn't wait to hear Kevin announce to the whole gym class that he was giving over his captainhood to me. I was about ready to burst while the man made Kevin's bagel. I'd never bought a gift for a boy, let alone a bagel that cost double what mine had.

As I approached the huge, crowded porch of Pepper, my panic over not finding Kevin multiplied 100 times when I spotted him immediately. He stood with two other boys who all had the same messy hair. I stuffed my partially eaten bagel in my pocket, wishing I had some water to wash it down, and walked up to them, holding the special wax paper-wrapped bagel in my hand.

"Veronica!" Kevin's blue eyes glowed and his whole face smiled.

"Hi, Kevin." I held out the bagel, not looking at his friends.

"What's this?"

"You shouldn't go without breakfast just because I won the bet."

"What bet?" one of his friends asked.

"I don't believe you," he said, ignoring his friend. He sniffed the bagel and grinned. "Lox. Come on, I'll walk you to homeroom."

He grabbed my hand right there in front of hundreds of people. I felt my pulse racing throughout my whole body. I couldn't focus on anything but pulling open the door and getting inside the building.

I said, "I had a really great time Saturday night." The bad things he'd said and the horrible feelings I'd had at the dance were gone for now. I'd deal with them later. Eventually I would ask him why his father was so prejudiced against black people.

"Me, too," he said. He reached in his pocket as we walked down the nearly empty hallway to our lockers on the second floor. He stopped and pulled out something shiny, but concealed it in his closed hand. "I want to give you something."

"What?"

"This is something I've had a long, long time, and now I want somebody special to have it." He opened his palm. In it was a silver two-inch key chain with the letters "KV" on it. "It's my initials, but I want to think of it as Kevin and Veronica."

He lifted it, making it dangle in the air between us. "Veronica, will you be my girl?"

I gulped. I'd seen a black and white movie where the boy asked the girl to be his "girl," and it sounded funny to hear Kevin ask me that way. His eyes widened and I realized he was waiting for my answer.

I nodded and said, "Uh-huh, I will."

Kevin exhaled.

I smiled so hard my eyes nearly squinted shut. I pulled my house key from my pocket and held it out to Kevin. "Will you do the honors?" Cap always said that to Daddy when she asked him to do something she didn't really want to do herself, like opening a jar of pickles or a bottle of wine.

"Sure." He twisted my key onto my new key chain.

"Too bad I don't have a strong necklace—I could dangle it from there," I said.

Kevin just smiled at me. I wanted to jump up and down and clap my hands.

The bell rang and he shook my hand. "So now it's official."

He leaned forward and his lips landed on mine. I closed my eyes and the next thing I knew, he was down the hall calling, "See you later."

I had a boyfriend! When I sat down in home-room, I only pretended to listen to Mrs. Jeffries' announcements. Actually, I was staring at the geometric design on the cover of my math book. I'd never noticed how pretty it was. I realized that a kaleidoscope picture in every color of the rainbow covered more than half of the front, the spine of the book, and all of the back. The purples and blue-greens made especially unique shades.

When I looked up, a boy I'd never talked to before was staring at me as I smiled at my math book. I turned up the corner of my mouth in what I hoped looked like a sneer. It happened again in Mrs. Green's class, only this time it was Jude Carver who was staring at me as I walked to my seat. I asked to go to the bathroom when the bell rang. I feared I had chunks of salt or poppy seeds from my bagel all over my face or between my teeth. In the bathroom mirror, I discovered that my skin was pink and dewy like I'd been sweating. I wiped my face with a wet paper towel and grinned at myself.

"I have a boyfriend," I mouthed to my reflec-tion. "Kevin, darling," I said out loud, then quickly checked the whole bathroom to make sure I was alone.

When I got back to class and sat in my seat, Jude leaned so close to my neck that I could feel his breath. "Do you have a fever?"

"No, I have a boyfriend," I whispered.

"What? I didn't hear you."

I wasn't sure if I'd really said that. I looked up toward Mrs. Green. She sat rigidly at her desk with one finger raised perpendicularly to her puckered lips. Jude and I weren't troublemakers, so she wasn't making us a public spectacle. I was glad Jude hadn't heard me boasting about Kevin—that might've hurt his feelings; after all, just a week ago he was the one making me have all those warm feelings. I felt the blood rushing through my body, pounding in my jugular more fiercely than ever. I somehow had to manage to sit still through reading and spelling.

Between first and second hours, I found Katie at her locker. "You didn't call," I said.

"My dad made us all have dinner together and be a family. It was really stupid. Allison puked, thank God, or we never would've gotten out of there. I didn't even do my homework this weekend, and it's all my dad and step-mom's fault."

I held up my new KV key chain.

Katie's mouth gaped. "Kevin Vogel? He gave you that?"

"He asked me to go with him," I squealed.

We grabbed each other by the elbows and jumped up and down. Katie stopped abruptly. "We're acting like sixth graders. We better control ourselves."

"I can't help it."

"Why hasn't Billy given me any presents?"

"Do your initials match like ours do?"

"Maggie McDougall says that when—"

"Please don't spoil my excitement with her words," I snapped.

"Wow, Veronica. You get a boyfriend and all of a sudden—"

"I'm sorry, Katie. It's just that I'm sure whatever I'm doing with Kevin wouldn't have anything to do with the Maggie McDougall way of thinking."

"For your information, I wasn't even going to say anything about you and your precious Kevin. I was going to say that Maggie says when a boy doesn't give you gifts, it's because he doesn't think he needs to win you over." Katie's eyes filled with tears. "I don't think Billy thinks he needs to win me over."

"I'm sorry. What can you do to make him see that he does need to win you over?"

She shrugged. "I have no idea. I guess I better ask Maggie."

The bell rang. We had ninety seconds to get to our next class.

"I really am happy for you," she said.

I felt warm and clammy and had a hard time concentrating all morning.

When lunch came, I was too restless to be hungry. I hadn't seen Kevin since before school. I didn't want to stand in the lunch line wondering what to do if I saw him or whether I should look for him. What if I saw him sitting on the opposite side of the cafeteria? What if I got separated from Katie walking into the cafeteria with my tray?

I found him standing at the end of the line, and I couldn't have been more thankful for such perfect timing; I didn't even have to cut. That left only one legitimate question remaining: where would we sit?

I walked up to Kevin and said, "Boo!" over his shoulder. He turned around and gave me a big smile. I noticed that his two front teeth overlapped each other. I wondered if he'd get braces. He reached out and grabbed my hand and squeezed it hard. I was positive that if he ever kissed me the way people kiss in the movies, I would faint and have to be rushed to the hospital.

We loaded our trays with food and paid. I followed Kevin into the cafeteria.

He asked, "So where do you want to sit?"

I gripped my tray carefully, fearing that a loss of concentration would cause me to drop the whole thing. The humiliating clanging and banging of a dropped lunchroom tray was not something I could handle at that moment in my life.

Looking around, I spotted my friends at our usual table and headed their way. Kevin followed. I started to introduce him to Susan and Debbie until I realized we all had gym together so they knew each other. As I took my first bite of pizza and washed it down with a sip of milk, I wondered if I would ever be calm around Kevin and other boys. I took a deep breath and told myself to loosen up, that he was just a boy who liked me. This made me smile at Kevin, who was staring at me across the table.

Kevin's friends sat down next to me and next to Kevin, including Billy, who for the first time sat by Katie.

He said, "Hey, man, since when do we sit over here?"

"The air is better over here," Kevin said.

Billy slugged Katie as a greeting, and I could tell by the way she didn't look at him that she was glad he was finally sitting with her. As he introduced his friends to me, more of our friends appeared, and before long, the whole table was full. I felt nervous and didn't say much; Kevin mostly talked to his friends and smiled at me.

After lunch, Kevin and I walked off alone toward his locker. I'd never been to his locker before, so when I saw a picture of the Detroit Red Wings taped to the inside, I figured they were the reason he was so good at hockey. Walking down the hall with him was like walking with Katie.

Except he's your boyfriend, the voice inside my head reminded me.

When we parted after the bell, he kissed my cheek and said, "See you in gym."

I walked to my locker wondering if he'd kissed any other girls.

In gym, I was sweating as I changed into shorts and a T-shirt. I'd stopped thinking about the black-white issue and now worried that I was going to have to perform athletically in front of Kevin. More importantly, I wondered if Kevin would follow through and hand over his captainhood to me in front of the whole class.

We assembled on our assigned spaces on the floor. Kevin sat three rows over and four spots behind me. Mrs. Dudda took roll. The captains were called up to select teams. Kevin stood and walked to the front of the class, straight up to Mrs. Dudda. She leaned toward him and he whispered into her ear. Sweat trickled down my back and under my arms. I wanted to disintegrate.

After about half a minute, Mrs. Dudda patted Kevin on the back and he walked back to his space. Mrs. Dudda turned to us. "Class, it has come to my attention that the captains have decided that in fairness to other students, new captains should be selected on a more frequent basis. I think that's a wonderful display, Kevin. Thank you for your generosity in your leadership position. Why don't you start this process by choosing your replacement?"

I couldn't believe it. All of a sudden I understood what it meant when a person was smooth. Kevin avoided humiliating himself in front of thirty-five other kids, and he also kept his end of the bet.

"Veronica," he called.

I was so stunned that the transfer of captainship happened so flawlessly and with the blessing of our gym teacher, that by the time I actually made eye contact with him, three other new captains had been selected, and no one thought it was a big deal at all.

I was in a daze as I selected my new team. Kevin got picked by another team before I made my first selection. Although I had been dreading the embarrassment I'd inevitably feel when Kevin picked me to replace him as captain, I was also anticipating the attention I'd get from my classmates when they realized that Kevin liked me so much he was handing over his reins to me.

I was so let down that all the captains got to do what Kevin did that I lost interest in being a team captain. Still, my team did okay, even when we played against the team Kevin was on.

By the end of gym, I wanted to corner Kevin and tell him it wasn't fair how he slithered out of his end of the bet. And yet I also wanted to congratulate him for being so clever. I didn't say anything at the end of class when he said he'd meet me at my locker after school. I was trying to decide if I should forget about gym and just confront him about the prejudice question. That was more important, anyway.

At the end of class, Mrs. Dudda announced that she had discussed it with the other gym teachers, and because of Kevin's suggestion, no single student would be captain of a team for more than a week; and each captain had the option of selecting his or her replacement. The fact that Kevin lost a bet with me over James's drums started a new gym class indoor games policy at Pepper.

Kevin beat me to my locker after school. I walked slowly down the hall as I built my courage. He leaned casually against my locker.

"Hey, Veronica," he called. "So did you have fun in gym or what?"

"I thought our bet was you were supposed to announce to the class that I was more qualified to be captain," I said. I did my combination quickly and pulled open the door.

"Well, I did, basically. You won the bet."

I looked at him, smiling because he was adorable as he bit his top lip enough to make him look even cuter. And guilty.

"Do you want to know the truth?" He stuffed his hands in his pockets. "I told Mrs. Dudda before class that I lost a bet and that I had to make you captain if she'd agree to it."

"Are you kidding?" I stared at him. I didn't know which story to believe. I felt a stab in my chest.

"No, I'm serious." His head was bowed down so low that he was practically looking up at me, though he was a few inches taller. "I started thinking today, what if Mrs. Dudda said I couldn't just hand over my captainhood to you? I was afraid she might say you're not qualified, and if she said that, I'd have to beat her up."

"I can't believe you did that."

"Are you mad at me?" He stuck out his bottom lip.

I shook my head. "No, I'm not mad at you. It would've been horrible if she'd said I wasn't qualified to be a captain in front of everybody. It was good of you to think ahead, I guess. You should know, though, that I got a presidential fitness award last year, so I'm pretty qualified to be captain of any gym team."

Kevin laughed. "They hand out those things to anybody!"

I punched his arm. "I earned it."

Kevin said, "Do you want to go to Pub?"

I nodded. Pub was a restaurant where couples hung out and had French fries and ice cream. I had never been to Pub with a boy.

As we headed for Pub, Kevin rambled on about something that happened to his friend's hand in shop, but other than the gory stuff, I wasn't paying attention. I was desperately trying to remember the sentences I'd planned to use when I told him I was black. I had to wait until the perfect time to bring it up.

As soon as he quits talking, I'll tell him.

He paused.

I pushed the button for the light to change at Nine Mile Road. I took a deep breath and said, "Kevin, I need for you to tell me more about what happened to your brother at Northland."

"You want to know the truth, or more of what I told you already?"

"Is there a difference?"

"We better not go to Pub if we're going to talk about this. Somebody might hear. Let's go to the park."

We walked in silence the few blocks to my house. Vicki wasn't home yet. I went inside and put my books on the dining room table while Kevin waited on the porch.

As soon as I walked back outside, he grabbed my hands. "Listen, you have to promise not to tell anybody what I tell you, okay? Not your parents or your sister or even Katie."

My stomach knotted and growled. I nodded. Was he going to be smooth again, or tell me the truth?

Halfway down the block, he spoke in a low voice, "My brother and my dad were at Northland. They split up and my brother saw my sister with this black guy, and he started yelling at her."

"Your brother started yelling in the middle of the mall?"

"Yes, but not at the black kid—at my sister. That's how the fight started. If my stupid dad hadn't been at Northland, my brother wouldn't have said anything but hi to my sister and the black guy. Marc was just afraid that my dad would see Sara and Al Newton and lose his temper right there and make a scene or something."

"That's terrible," I said. I felt relieved that Kevin's brother was fighting with his sister. Now I knew that the fight hadn't been what the news had called it: *racially motivated.*

Kevin continued. "Nobody even hit Marc. He tripped and fell back on his hand and that's how he broke his fingers. That was when my dad came up to him. By then Sara had left. Marc told her she better leave fast because he was meeting Dad any minute. My dad took Marc to the emergency room after that and they fixed his fingers."

"Oh, Kevin," I said with a gush of breath, "I am so glad you told me all of this. I was so afraid that you were prejudiced, with all that stuff you said at the dance about black people being bad. But every time you said something, you said that was what your dad thought—I was hoping that it really was what he thought, and not what you thought."

"My brother and sister and I all have black friends. It's true what I said about not being able to bring them over to my house, or my dad will throw a fit. He can be a real jerk sometimes. I don't think my dad will ever let us bring black kids over. He's always threatening to beat our butts, like he did Sara, so we obey him. We don't have a choice."

"Your father sounds mean."

"He's okay, I guess. I don't talk to him that much."

"Kevin, I have to tell you that during the dance I was afraid to have you meet my mother after what you said. Now I'm positive that you can handle it."

"Handle what?"

"My mother is black."

He stopped walking. "What are you talking about? How can your mom be black when your eyes are blue and your skin is white?"

"My father is white. I just happened to turn out this way. My mother is black."

"But, Veronica, you're *so* white." He pinched my cheek, laughing. "Are you sure you weren't adopted?"

"Quit." I swatted his hand away. I didn't want him kidding around when I was being so serious. Staring into his bright eyes, I tried to understand what his reaction was, uncertain whether his feelings had changed toward me in the last seconds.

"That's really cool. I can't wait to meet your mom."

"Isn't that funny how sometimes you just don't know?"

"Yeah. I'm dating a black girl and I didn't even know it." He put his arm around me and we started walking again.

As we walked on in silence, I began to worry. Was he being sincere? Or smooth?

After about two minutes, he told me that his math teacher had yelled at a really dumb kid who'd earned an "E triple minus" on his test and that he was going to flunk math if he didn't start applying himself. I felt horribly unsettled but glad that he'd started talking about something else.

We reached the park and sat on the swings, not talking, until all of a sudden Kevin said, "Race ya!"

He pushed himself off the ground and made his swing go so high I thought he'd flip over the top of the swing set. I couldn't get as high as him, but I laughed as we pretended to race each other through the air.

Kevin yelled, "Jump off!" He flew through the air as his swing slumped limply behind him, the chain clinking in on itself. He landed on his hands and knees about twenty feet forward on the wood chips scattered over the ground. I let my feet hit the ground to slow myself down, glad I was wearing tennis shoes. He wasn't hurt, just dirty. He wiped his hair out of his eyes and smeared dirt on his forehead in the process.

He asked, "Why'd you chicken out?"

"I didn't chicken out. I didn't want to get dirty."

"Am I a mess?"

"You're okay." I laughed nervously, a high-pitched fake laugh that echoed in my mind as we walked away from the park.

Kevin hadn't said anything nice to me of any significance since learning I was black. I feared the worst, but I didn't want to confirm it by asking him if anything was wrong.

When we reached a halfway point between our houses, I invited him over to meet Cap and Daddy, but he said he'd better get home. I wanted to believe nothing had changed, but I felt so worried and queasy that I couldn't eat dinner.

I called Kevin at eight-thirty, planning to hang up if his father answered. By some miracle, Kevin answered. "I just wanted to make sure I don't have to bring you a bagel tomorrow," I said.

He laughed and said, "Of course not. You won the bet. Besides, you're the new captain."

I guessed that meant nothing had changed.

THE END

About the Author

CATHERINE MARIE ATKINS GREENSPAN has been writing books since she was five. A Michigan native, she has lived in California, Nevada, Oregon, Idaho, and Tennessee. These days, she calls the Land of Enchantment home.

CPSIA information can be obtained
at www.ICGtesting.com
Printed in the USA
FFOW04n0104190518
46767348-48915FF